How Many Hugs?

For Graham —H.S.

For b, who gives the best hugs of all :: - —S.H.

♥

A FEIWEL AND FRIENDS BOOK

An imprint of Macmillan Publishing Group, LLC
175 Fifth Avenue, New York, NY 10010

Our books may be purchased in bulk for promotional, educational, or business use. Please contact your local
bookseller or the Macmillan Corporate and Premium Sales Department at (800) 221-7945 ext. 5442 or by e-mail at
MacmillanSpecialMarkets@macmillan.com.

Library of Congress Cataloging-in-Publication Data is available.

ISBN 978-1-250-06651-0

Book design by Eileen Savage

Feiwel and Friends logo designed by Filomena Tuosto

First Edition—2017
The illustrations for this book began as pencil drawings on Bienfang marker paper, which
were then scanned and painted digitally in Corel Painter 2015 using modified Impasto brushes.

1 3 5 7 9 10 8 6 4 2

mackids.com

How Many Hugs?

Heather Swain

Illustrated by Steven Henry

Feiwel and Friends
New York

Since snakes have no arms, nor any feet,
they can slither about very discreet.

But this lack of appendages surely would make
an awkward affair of a hug from a snake.

Clams have a foot to push through the sand
but not enough leg on which to stand.

A hug from a clam would be more like a pinch
from their hard little shells opened an inch.

Giving nice hugs takes two
legs or two arms
to wrap up a loved one all
snuggly warm.

So, if each pair of arms
can give a nice hug,
how many hugs could
you get from a bug?

A bug has six arms so baby bug gets three.

Three sweet hugs from its bug daddy.

Eight-legged critters, known as arachnids, give four excellent embraces to their eight-legged kids.

Scorpions, spiders, ticks, and mites wrap up their wee ones in four squeezy delights.

And down in the ocean an
octopus waits
to wrap up its loves in two
fours, which is eight.

That's eight arms like the
spider, but here it gets odd.
An octopus is not an
arachnid—it's a cephalopod.

Horseshoe crabs have twelve
arms, six on each side.

That's six grasping appendages
to open up wide.

Even better, a giant isopod has
fourteen—that's seven and seven
to step in between.

Don't be fooled by the shrimp's
shrimpy name.
Those little sea critters give great
hugs all the same.

With twenty arms, their hugs are a ten.
That's ten times the hugs, time and again.

Think we're done? It's not time to settle! Not till we've hugged the lovely sea nettle.

With twenty-eight arms, this jellyfish is bold when it wraps its lovey in a fourteen-hug hold.

The sunflower sea star can give
twenty embraces
with up to forty legs it drapes
over places.

While nautilus—a small secretive squid that lives in a chamber where she likes to stay hid—comes out for a squeeze from

her ninety long tentacles.
That's forty-five hugs, each one identical.

Centipedes, those crawliest bugs,
have 300 legs for giving out hugs.
That's 150 on one side to grasp
and 150 on the other to clasp.

Comparatively speaking, that isn't so nifty because her millipede cousin has seven hundred fifty.

That's three hundred seventy-five squinches and scrunches from millipede mamas that love babies bunches.

So how many hugs could I give to you?
I have only two arms—you know that
it's true.

Here's a hug for each bird in the sky
and fish in the sea,
all the critters on earth and bugs in
the trees.

If you add all those up, it's over a
billion, but each hug from you is one
in a million.

Fun Facts

Since snakes have no arms or legs, they use their muscles and scales to slither from side to side (serpentine movement), inch themselves forward (concertina movement), or zigzag up a sandy hill (sidewinding). Flying snakes fling themselves from trees and glide through the air.

Clams, oysters, and mussels are bivalves. They have a two-part hinged shell that covers their soft bodies and a muscle called a foot that they use to pull themselves across sand or mud. They mostly live in the ocean, but some live in fresh water, too.

Insects, or what we like to call bugs, have three body parts and six legs. Most also have antennae and wings (like flies, moths, butterflies, bees, and dragonflies). Some don't have wings (such as lice, fleas, and silverfish). Insects make up 85% of all life-forms on earth!

Spiders, ticks, mites, and scorpions are all eight-legged creatures. They are not insects. Their scientific name is Arachnida.

An octopus is a cephalopod that lives in the ocean. It has eight limbs (six that function like arms plus two that function more like legs), three hearts, and blue blood. If an octopus loses one of its limbs, it can grow another one.

Horseshoe crabs live in sand and mud in shallow ocean water. They are closely related to spiders and scorpions, but they have a hard shell (or carapace) plus five pairs of walking legs and two claws for a total of 12 appendages.

The giant isopod is related to shrimp and crabs from the ocean and pill bugs from your garden. They have seven pairs of legs and a hard shell. Like pill bugs, they roll into a ball to protect themselves when in danger.

Shrimp and prawns are crustaceans that live in the ocean. Like other crustaceans, they have an exoskeleton. They also have five pairs of swimming legs and five pairs of walking legs. When in danger they can propel themselves backward.

Sea nettles are a type of jellyfish, which are soft, nearly transparent sea creatures without brains or eyes. They use poisonous barbs (called nematocysts) on their tentacles to capture prey and protect themselves.

Despite their pretty name, sunflower sea stars are large, excellent hunters. They use tiny tube feet on the bottoms of their arms to move quickly across the ocean floor. Most have 16–24 tentacles, but some have up to 40 arms, which can regrow if lost.

The chambered nautilus is related to the squid and the octopus, but unlike those creatures, it has a hard shell and more than 90 tentacles. The nautilus uses a small tube (called a siphon) to expel water and propel itself through the ocean quickly.

The word *centipede* means "hundred legs," but this is not accurate. Centipedes have one pair of legs on each body segment. Each time they molt, they add a new body segment with more legs. Each new set of legs is longer than the one before it. Since centipedes have more than three body segments, they are not bugs or insects. They are called Chilopoda. There are many different kinds of centipedes, which can have from 30 to 350 legs.

Millipedes are similar to centipedes, but they have two pairs of legs on each body segment and can have up to 750 legs! Unlike centipedes, which hunt for prey, millipedes only eat decaying plants.